Jam Session

Tiger Woods

Terri Dougherty

ABDO Publishing Company

visit us at
www.abdopub.com

Published by ABDO Publishing Company, 4940 Viking Drive, Suite 622, Edina, Minnesota 55435.
Copyright © 1999 by Abdo Consulting Group, Inc. International copyrights reserved in all countries.
No part of this book may be reproduced in any form without written permission from the publisher.

Printed in the United States.

Cover and Interior Photo credits: AP/Wide World Photos

Edited by Denis Dougherty

Sources: Golf Digest; Los Angeles Times; People Magazine; Sport Magazine; Sports Illustrated; Sports Illustrated For Kids; USA Today

Library of Congress Cataloging-in-Publication Data

Dougherty, Terri.
    Tiger Woods / Terri Dougherty.
        p.   cm. -- (Jam Session)
    Includes index.
    Summary: Presents a biography of the professional golfer, who at the age of twenty-one, became the first person of color and the youngest player to win the Masters Golf Tournament.
    ISBN 1-57765-041-7 (hardcover)
    ISBN 1-57765-343-2 (paperback)
    1. Woods, Tiger--Juvenile literature.   2. Golfers--United States--Biography--Juvenile literature.
    [1. Woods, Tiger. 2. Golfers. 3. Racially mixed people--Biography.] I. Title. II. Series.
    GV964.WW66D68   1999
    796.352'092--dc21
    [b]   98-24548
                                              CIP
                                               AC

Contents

The Young Master

*T*iger Woods was burning up the course in the 1997 Masters tournament at Augusta National.

He swung his golf club and controlled his shots perfectly. Over and over again, his drives went down the middle of the fairway. On the putting greens, he had just the right touch.

Tiger was in a zone. The crowds and his opponents were awed.

"Tiger is out there playing another game. This is a golf course that he's going to own for a long time," said Jack Nicklaus, who is considered to be the best golfer ever. "He's going to win here a lot."

When it was over, he had done more than win the tournament. He set six Masters records. At 21, he was the youngest Masters champion ever. He finished golf's most prestigious tournament with an 18-under-par 270, the best Masters score anyone ever had! He also won by 12 strokes, the largest Masters margin of victory.

"My first nine Thursday, I was like anyone else—nervous," Tiger said. "But from there it evolved into one of the best ball-striking, putting, and management rounds I've ever put together."

After Tiger made his final putt, he gave his father and mother a big hug. The previous night, his father had told him, "Son, this is going to be one of the toughest rounds you've ever had to play. But if you'll be yourself, it'll be one of the most rewarding you've ever played."

"He was right," Tiger said.

Tiger's Masters victory confirmed what people had been saying about him since he was six years old: Tiger was a lion on the golf course.

Tiger Woods sinks a putt at the Masters.

Golf Cub

*T*iger Woods wasn't born with a golf club in his hands, but he has been holding one since he was practically a baby. When he was six months old, he began watching his father hit practice shots into a net in the family garage.

"He didn't make any noise," Tiger's father, Earl Woods, said. "He was totally engrossed in my hitting balls. By the time he was 10 months, he had to be fed in there."

Before Tiger was a year old, his father cut down a putter and Tiger started hitting the ball into the net himself.

"He was hitting the ball on target," his father said.

When Tiger was two, he won a local pitch, putt, and drive competition for kids age 10 and under. His earliest golf memory is bringing home a big trophy from a local junior tournament when he was only four years old.

"He had talent oozing out of his fingertips," said Rudy Duran, a professional golfer who began coaching Tiger when he was four.

When Tiger was five, he competed against 17-year-olds in junior competitions and was featured on the TV show, "That's Incredible." By age six, he had his first hole-in-one.

"Even as a little boy, Tiger was very organized about his preparation," Duran said. "He didn't want to rush into an event, he wanted to ease into it calmly. When it was really time to do it, he was confident and patient because he knew he was most prepared."

Tiger's father took him to golf courses often. Earl helped Tiger learn to concentrate by jingling coins while the boy lined up his shot.

"His father was a great role model," golf pro Keith McDuff said. "He taught him that you get out of life what you put into it—on the course and off."

Tiger's dad gave him his nickname. Earl Woods had been in the military in Vietnam, and served with a South Vietnamese officer whose nickname was Tiger. Tiger had saved Earl Woods' life, so Earl gave his son the same nickname out of gratitude.

Tiger's real name, Eldrick, was given to him by his mother, Kultida. It is comprised of letters from the names of his parents.

Kultida is from Thailand, and met Earl while he was serving in the military there. Tiger is proud of his heritage, and has a foundation that promotes minority participation in golf. His ancestors are African American, Thai, Chinese, Native American, and white. He enjoys being a role model for minorities.

"I accept that role," Tiger said. "I've accepted that since I was a very little boy. I like the fact that I can influence people with my game in a positive way."

Tiger was winning tournaments by age four and had his first hole-in-one at six years old.

On the Prowl

When Tiger was 10, he had a list of the major championships won by golf legend Jack Nicklaus taped near his bed so he could measure his own progress.

Tiger had already established himself as a top golfer. At age eight, he won the first of six age-group titles at the Optimist Junior World tournaments. His coach thought he was destined for big things.

"By then I thought he probably could be the best player in the world one day," Duran said.

At the age of 13, Tiger played a round of golf with pro John Daly in the 1989 Big I Classic. Daly beat him by only a stroke, and Tiger's score beat eight of 20 pros in the tournament.

"He played like he was 18 or 19," Daly recalled. "He had all the tools, and he was very disciplined."

The next year, Tiger finished second in the PGA Junior and was a semifinalist in the U.S. Junior. The following season, Tiger did something no 15-year-old had ever done: He won the U.S. Junior Amateur tournament.

By the time he was a freshman in high school, Tiger was already a seasoned golfer. Some thought he might get tired of the game, but he never did. Tiger took a break when he got bored, but usually loved to practice.

"Golf never wears me down," Tiger said.

Tiger attended Western High in Anaheim, California. He was the first freshman to capture the California high school championship and won the Los Angeles Junior Golfing Championship.

Tiger at age 15 with father, Earl, and mother, Kultida.

"Tiger would go out to the club and hit balls for three hours," his high school coach, Don Crosby, remembered. "In the end there is no gimmick. If you hit 10,000 balls you're going to get good at the game."

Tiger also did well with his schoolwork.

"I try to get Tiger to read, but never have to push," Earl Woods said. "He is totally self-responsible. I never ask him if his homework is done. He learns that discipline from golf. When he was a little boy, I asked him, 'Who's responsible for you missing that shot? Was it the club? Was it the noise? No, it was you. And it's your responsibility to do your lesson, isn't it?' That's it. He got it right there."

Tiger set his goals on par with a basketball superstar.

"I want to be the Michael Jordan of golf," Tiger once said.

Young Tiger Woods practicing in Cypress, California.

Playing with the Pros

When Tiger was only a teenager, he could hit the ball long and high. He was accurate when he got close to the hole. He kept his composure on the course.

These attributes helped him become the first golfer to win the U.S. Junior twice. His parents had boxes of his golf trophies stored in their garage in Cypress, about 35 miles (56 km) southwest of Los Angeles.

"I want to be the best golfer ever," Tiger said. "I don't know whether I'll achieve it or not. I think I'd be more worried if I set too low a goal and achieved it too easily."

In 1992, Tiger had the opportunity to play in his first professional tournament, although he was still an amateur. When Tiger teed it up in the Los Angeles Open, he became the youngest golfer to play in a PGA Tour event.

"I was so tense I had a tough time holding the club," said Tiger, who was 16 years and 2 months old. "It was like rigor mortis had set in."

The crowd loved him. Fans shouted "You the kid!" He walked onto the final green to a rousing ovation.

It was the first time Tiger had a large crowd of people watching him, and it distracted him.

"I've never had a gallery," Tiger said. "I wasn't used to it."

Tiger played two rounds and finished at five over par. His score was six shots too high for him to continue to play in the tournament.

"It was a learning experience," Tiger said. "And I learned I'm not that good."

But he showed he could compete with the best.

"He plays the mental game like he's been out there seven or eight years," veteran caddie Ron Matthews said.

"I've got a lot of growing to do, both physically and mentally," Tiger said, "but I'll play these guys again—eventually."

Tiger hitting an approach shot.

Coming Out of the Woods

*I*n 1993, Tiger had a chance to set another record. He could become the first golfer to win three straight U.S. Junior Amateur titles.

He trailed Ryan Armour by two strokes with two holes left. On the 17th and 18th holes, Tiger made birdies. This sent him into a playoff with Ryan.

On the next hole, Tiger made a par putt to win the tournament!

"It was the most amazing comeback of my career," Tiger said. "I had to play the best two holes of my life under the toughest circumstances, and I did it."

After Tiger sank his winning putt, he cried. His dad ran onto the green and hugged him.

"All Tiger could say was, 'I did it, I did it,' " Earl Woods said, "and I kept saying, 'I'm so proud of you' over and over. Time stops in moments like that."

Tiger didn't let his good play go to his head. He realized he still had a lot to learn.

"He tells me all the time that he's got a long way to go," Earl Woods said. "And I say, 'Yes, you do.' If he wasn't aware of this, he would be cocky, arrogant, and inexperienced. But he acknowledges that things are going to be tougher as he gets older."

In 1994, Tiger's goal was to win the adult U.S. Amateur tournament. Once again, he was behind heading into the final holes. He trailed Trip Kuehne by five shots with 13 holes to play at the Sawgrass Tournament Players Club in Ponte Verde Beach, Florida.

Then he staged the greatest comeback in the history of the U.S. Amateur Golf Championship.

On the 16th hole, Tiger made birdie to pull even with Trip. On the next hole, the ball took a hop and stopped inches from the water. It was 12 feet (3.7 m) from the hole. Tiger made the birdie putt. That put him ahead!

"You know you have to do it and you go ahead and do it," Tiger said. "It's a great feeling."

Tiger Woods at Stanford in 1994

Driving to Stardom

A month after Tiger won his first U.S. Amateur tournament, he enrolled at Stanford University in Northern California. He majored in economics, and played on the golf team.

He also played in the Masters, practicing with golfing greats Nick Faldo, Greg Norman, and Fred Couples. He was composed and self-assured, and placed 41st in the tournament. The next year, he won his second U.S. Amateur tournament.

Tiger played in his third U.S. Amateur tournament in 1996. He was down by five strokes with 16 holes left. During the lunch break, he went to the practice range with his coach.

His strategy worked, and with two holes left he was down by only two strokes. Then, after eight hours of golf, it came down to a sudden death hole between Tiger and Steve Schott.

Tiger hit an 18-inch (46 cm) par putt to win!

After he won, Tiger's mother ran onto the green. He hugged her. Then he hugged his father, who was so happy he cried.

"Against Tiger Woods, no lead is secure," Schott said.

"I've played better in my life," Tiger said. "But I've never been in this situation where I've played so well."

Tiger Woods holds his trophy after winning the U.S. Amateur Championship in 1995.

A Tiger of a Different Stripe

*A*fter winning his third U.S. Amateur title, Tiger decided it was time to turn pro. He tied for 60th in his first professional tournament, the Greater Milwaukee Open, and went on to win two of the first seven events he entered.

"That was my goal," Tiger said, referring to winning on the pro tour, "and I accomplished it."

Tiger had already earned the respect of some of the biggest names in golf.

Golf legends Arnold Palmer (L) and Jack Nicklaus (C) agree that Tiger is on his way to being one of the greatest golfers ever.

"Arnold (Palmer) and I both agreed you could take all his Masters and all mine, and Tiger could win more than both of us put together before he's done," Nicklaus said after playing a practice round with Tiger at the 1996 Masters.

"He is absolutely the finest, most fundamentally sound golfer I have ever seen, at almost any age."

Tiger Woods at the 1997 Mercedes Championships.

Masterful

*T*iger knew he would be in the spotlight in his biggest pro tournament so far: the Masters at Augusta National in Augusta, Georgia. He had played the course before, as an amateur, and the week before the tournament he immersed himself in golf.

For three days he practiced with his coach, and for four days he practiced alone. At the end of the week, he played a great round with Mark O'Meara, his best friend on the tour. He went to Augusta expecting to win.

Unlike many of the other tournaments Tiger won, he didn't have to come from behind. After three rounds, he had a nine-stroke lead, the biggest in 61 Masters tournaments.

The gallery at the Masters was in awe of Tiger's shots and his final score.

"Granted it's a big lead, (but) I need to go out and shoot a pretty good number," Tiger said before his final round. "I need to drive well, think well, play well."

Tiger did play well, and became the youngest person ever to win the traditional green jacket given to the winner of the Masters. He was also the first African American to win at Augusta.

Even President Clinton was excited about Tiger's win and called him on the phone.

"He said he was proud of the way I played," Tiger said. "He said the best shot he saw all week was the shot of me hugging my dad."

After his Masters win, Tiger had to learn to deal with his celebrity status.

"I was at home the other day and I went into Subway just to pick up a sandwich," Tiger said. "My best friend went there after I did, and the whole talk of the shopping center was, 'Tiger Woods was in Subway.' I never had to deal with that."

Tiger wins the Masters and takes home the green jacket.

He misses practicing in peace and going out to dinner without being bothered.

"But then, there are some perks to being who I am ... doing the things I like to do," Tiger said. "I wouldn't trade that."

Tiger Tamed

After Tiger won the Masters, players and fans wondered if he would be able to win the next major tournament: The U.S. Open at Congressional Country Club in Bethesda, Maryland.

"He's the guy to beat, no question," tour pro Paul Goydos said.

But Tiger shot six over par and finished tied for 19th.

"This course wore me out," Tiger said. "I hit some good shots and I hit some bad shots. It took its toll on me. It humbled me. It humbled me big time and that's just the way it is.

"My mind was tested," Tiger said. "My patience, my grit, every kind of emotion you can conjure up was tested this week. I think I held up pretty good, but I could have held up better.

"I learned a lot," he added. "This golf course beat me up."

It's not unusual for some of the world's best golfers to go years without winning a major tournament. But everyone expected so much out of Tiger. Although he placed near the top in several tournaments, when he didn't win big tournaments questions were raised about his ability. But Tiger remained calm.

"Golf humbles you every day, every shot, really," he said. "I know how hard the game is."

He still sets his goals high.

"I expect to win every tournament I play because that's what I go there to do," Tiger said.

Tiger slumps on the third green during the final round of the U.S. Open.

Out of the Rough

*T*iger once again prepared diligently for the Masters in 1998. He secluded himself at his home in Isleworth, outside Orlando, Florida. He didn't accept calls. He didn't play video games with his friends. He didn't do interviews.

He thought about his game and played the course in his head.

"Tiger's favorite thing has always been getting ready, preparing for a major," Earl Woods said. "He is an analytical, systems-oriented person, and that's how he likes to manage his golf."

Tiger worked on adding muscle to his 6-foot-2, 170-pound frame.

"Tiger has gotten incredibly strong for a golfer," Tiger's coach, Butch Harmon, said. "It has given him a very stable base, which makes it easier for him to repeat his swing."

Tiger tied for eighth in the Masters, shooting three-under-par. He was six shots behind winner and friend O'Meara.

Although he was struggling through a 10-month slump, failing to win any tournaments on the PGA Tour, Tiger kept his focus. He wasn't down about his chances.

"I go to each tournament with the intention of winning," he said. "But someone else playing well isn't going to change my way of playing. I still practice hard, do everything the same. (Winning) is a matter of being at the right place at the right time.

"I've been right there," Tiger said. "I just haven't been able to get that one shot here or there to win it. I have been in the hunt much of the time. It's just a matter of shooting that one round that gets you over the hump."

Then in May 1998, Tiger ended his championship drought by winning the BellSouth Classic in Duluth, Georgia, by one stroke. With Tiger's tremendous talent and determined attitude, it was only a matter of time before he got out of the rough.

Tiger Woods smiles as he holds the trophy after winning the BellSouth Classic.

Eldrick "Tiger" Woods Profile

Born: December 30, 1975

Hometown: Cypress, CA

Family: Father, Earl; mother, Kultida; two half-brothers, Kevin and Earl Jr.; half-sister, Royce.

Lives: Isleworth, Florida.

Height: 6 feet 2 inches

Weight: 170 pounds

Nickname: Tiger, after a friend of his father.

Personal: Likes to play video games, go fishing, and watch and play basketball and baseball. His favorite teams are the Los Angeles Lakers and the Chicago Bulls. Cheeseburgers, fries, and steak are his favorite foods, with strawberry milk shakes for dessert. He likes to listen to rap and rhythm and blues. "Life and Times of Frederick Douglass," by Frederick Douglass, is his favorite book.

Chronology

1975 - Born December 30.

1976 - Started hitting golf balls.

1978 - Won local pitch, putt, and drive competition.

1981 - Featured on TV show "That's Incredible."

1982 - Makes a hole-in-one.

1984 - Won first of six Optimist Junior World Championships.

1991 - Won U.S. Junior Amateur title.

1992 - Won U.S. Junior Amateur title. Won American Junior Golf Association's Player of the Year Award. Competed in first PGA tournament, the Los Angeles Open, as an amateur.

1993 - Won U.S. Junior Amateur title.

1994 - Graduated from Western High School in Anaheim, California.
Won U.S. Amateur title.
Starts college at Stanford.

1995 - Won U.S. Amateur title.

1996 - Won U.S. Amateur title.
Turns pro and won two of his first seven PGA Tour events.
Selected as Sports Illustrated's "Sportsman of the Year."

1997 - Won Masters tournament.
Became youngest golfer
to achieve No. 1 world
ranking at age
21 years, 24 weeks.
Named The
Associated Press
Male Athlete of
the Year.

Awards and Honors

U.S. Junior Amateur champion - 1991, 1992, 1993

U.S. Amateur champion - 1994, 1995, 1996

Sports Illustrated "Sportsman of the Year" - 1996

Masters tournament winner - 1997

The Associated Press Male Athlete of the Year - 1997

Glossary

AMATEUR - An athlete who plays his or her sport as a hobby rather than as a profession.

BIRDIE - A score of one shot under par on a single hole.

DRIVE - A shot hit from the tee.

HOLE - A numbered section of the golf course, including a tee, fairway and green. Also, the circular cup into which the golfer hits a ball.

HOLE-IN-ONE - Making the ball go into the hole with one shot.

PAR - The score a player is expected to make on an individual hole or on a certain course.

PGA - Professional Golfers' Association.

PRO - A person who earns a living at a sport.

PUTT - Shot made on the green area, close to the hole, with a putter.

ROUGH - A part of the golf course where grass and weeds grow uncut.

STROKE - To swing at a golf ball. In golf, your score is measured by the number of strokes it takes you to complete a course.

Index